OH!! MAN...IYA

About Men

Shirish Pawar

CONTENTS

Preface

The book is not exactly a sequel of Oh!! Womaniya but it speaks about the other gender on the earth. After writing about women it almost became my responsibility to write about men.

Male – Men are not much spoken about, we have always shown concern to women than men. While women always receive applause for being good wife and mother, husband hardly gets it. There is no idea of comparing these two genders as they are the best on their own but together they do wonders. Thou we always hold them opposite to each other they are collectively a miracle. The book cover reflects the magic of them being one.

Men have always been looked upon as the responsible person in the family; unknowingly he is bought up with a great responsibility and with sense of being the whole and sole of the family. Thou today women are no more lagging behind still men are looked upon to be stronger gender. He has his softer, fragile side which needs to be taken care of or say attended.

Being women it was easy to write Oh Womaniya, but it was equally difficult to write about Men as we look at them differently. I have tried my best to make justice to them.

SPECIAL THANKS AND COURTESY TO :-

Kindle, Google and online pictures and/or figures at public domain which may be helpful to many reader to connect to author's thoughts. There is no intention to harm or cause injury to any individual, institution, or group as pictures are obtained from the public domain, if any of the said pictures and/or figures are copyright please let us know and we certainly tender credit in next edition.

Disclaimer :-

The book is based on fiction any characters, circumstances, situations and the stories of the book are the author's self imagination and creation. Any similarity and/or resemblance of the story to individual, institution, or group living or dead is mere a co-incident and author is not liable for any consequences or result arise out of it.

MAN...N KI BAAT

W omen dream of a prince charming on a white horse who comes all across the mountains and seas just to save her, love her. Many women are born with this dream to target the prince.

On the other side of the world are we – Men born like any other child on earth, naked crying for disturbing from comfort zone and exposing to sudden human world with lots and lots of clear chaos heard. Sometimes, a pat on the bum by a human being wearing mask. Our birth is celebrated as the one of carrier of genes who holds the responsibility of carrying those genes with name to other healthy generation. Remember the famous character Virus- Viru Shahastrabuddhe from three idiots when got rid of engineers in his life and asked the new born kid in his hand if he

wants to be a footballer? Within next few minutes of birth.
As a kid they see people always keeping hopes from them as and when they feel. Being a boy they are taught they should not cry like girls. They even forget it that he is just a child, who needs to express and cry out.

The awareness program is conducted by society around them, as they grow up they understand they have different rules to follow in their life just because he is a man. When society felt a woman was most vulnerable species, men were crushed behind the abla nari concept. Gender equality came just for the sake of women and men have no say on it. A girl marries thinking he is the shining armour she dreamt of, but as it is not a bookish fairy tale and he is a human being with difference and limitations, after some days when women realises this they will feel fooled for no reason.
Men are simple with few basic needs-lets talk about happiness and joy; there are two segments like what makes them happy and how they express their happiness.
Like any other human being a nice music, good food, smiling, welcoming faces, good looks, or if anyone praises those boosts confidence and makes them feel happy.

To express feelings like happiness joy they prefer to do it physically then verbally. Unlike, women who express verbally most of the times. Men may not say it; they will smile, hug or just pat your back for good job.

Men are bad at reading minds, especially women's; giving subtle hints to them doesn't work with them. Like if you want help, or want them to do something you will have to say it. They will approach you only when you call them for help, else they are under impression that you are loving your job and all is well at your end. When men are stressed out they prefer to be alone, just playing a video game, watching television or just resting quietly. Unlike women who always want to discuss everything about anything, Men prefer to stay alone, and come up with some solution in such situations.

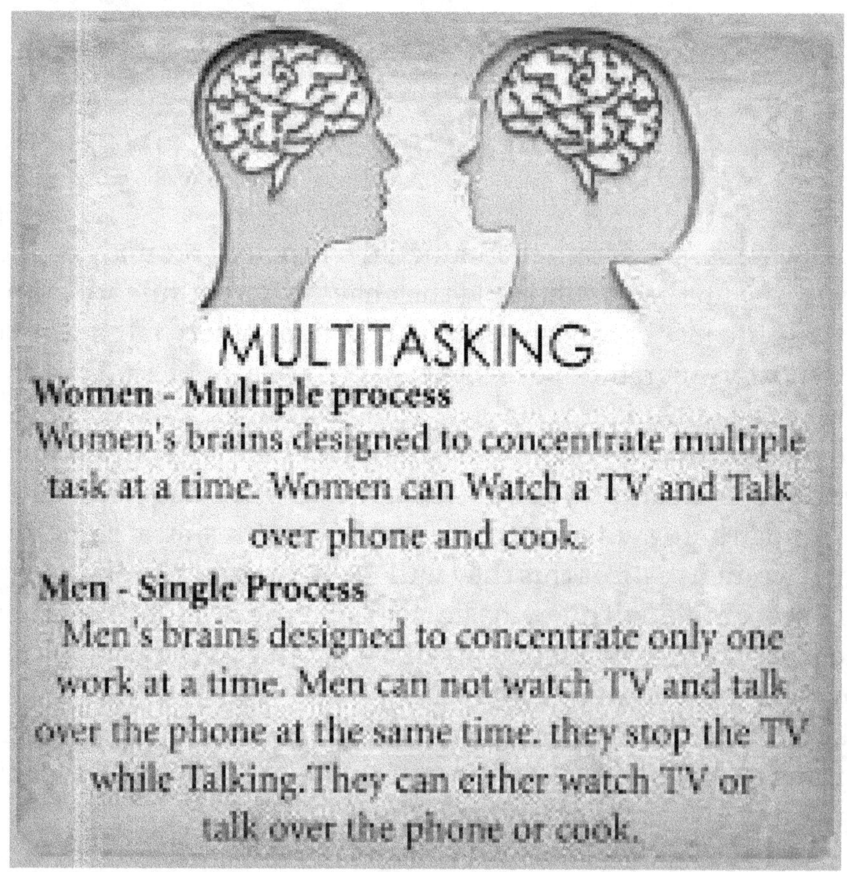

Men are not good at multitasking, yes they do not hear you if they are watching television or hearing to some music. They cannot keep an eye on kid if they busy over phone or in some work. It may give women a feeling of ignorance or not loved anymore but the fact is they are busy and not multitasking. You need to stand in front of them ask them to listen to you and then expect him to listen.

Men do not say often how much they love, for them love is more physical and logical. They prefer to say it once and once it is done you know it for life time, where as women need reassurance of love and care from time to time. They prefer helping you in household, seeking advice and spending time than expressing love verbally.

Like any other human on earth men also prefer to have their own space, they also need the so called me time and get irritated if they are not given it, or if someone intrudes.

Men appreciate women who are independent, and have their space in life. They would appreciate you if you seek an opinion, or ask for direction etc, like a guide. They would always recommend you to be self sufficient and not dependable.

Most of the men are mommas boy's like women's are "Papa ki pari". It is ok to be one, as she is the first women in his life who loves him to no end. But that doesn't compare his love to any other female in his life. In fact if you want to see how good the guy is, always watch him when he is with his mother or sisters. That will give you an idea of real 'HE'

RAVANA-THE TEN HEADED DEMON

Dasshera the day when good won over evil, we celebrate it every year. Lord Ram is glorified and people have hatred for Ravana. Lord Ram was the incarnation of Vishnu and he had taken a human birth to kill Ravana.

Ravana is believed to most revered devotee of Shiva, one of the greatest scholars and efficient rulers. He is the multi headed king of Lanka with ten heads and twenty arms. He could easily change into any form he wished. We do not respect Ravana for the fact that he abducted Sita.

He was a great king and loving brother. It was his act of revenge against the insult of his sister Shurpanakha that brought his downfall. He never violated Sita's integrity. Being an illusionist he could have easily made Sita fall for him, but his humanity kept him from doing so. He was great in capabilities in terms of strength, intellect and devotion,

He was born to couple father Vishwasrao a rishi of Pulastya Clan and Mother Kaikasi who belonged to demon clan, hence he was half Brahmin and half demon, with proficiency a Brahmin would possess and immense power a demon would possess.

He had immense knowledge of all four Vedas and Upanishads, and had knowledge in field of medicine too. He was amazing veena player. He was gifted a sword by Lord Shiva, when Ravan Sang the Shiv Tandav for praising him

At the time of battle between Rama and Ravana, a Brahmin could not be found to perform the yagya. Ravana being half Brahmin performed the ritual-Yagna favouring both sides for the battle that was fought to destroy him.

Ravana is neither the demon as he is not portrayed nor is he a hero. There is a blurred line between the good and evil Ravana.

LETTER TO WIFE

In marriage both wife and husband are equal. Only that wife is more vocal about their emotions and needs than men. Husbands are bit reluctant to express themselves. Men are more accommodative than women. They both need each other's support, may it be financial emotional or physical.

Here is letter for wife

There is no comparison between you and my mom. You both have a definite place in my heart. Do not feel ignored if I sit with mom for longer time or spend more time with her. I love both of you equally please do not give me a choice to select one from two of you as I cannot do it.

I do not express my feeling often like you do, but when I appreciate your food, when I compliment you, just hug you for nothing, please understand it is my love for you. When I get a gift or surprise for you for no reason it is just because I care I love, I am concerned.

I am always listening to you after a long day. No matter how I tired I am I m listening, When I say yes or no as a response to your talks it does not mean I am not interested or I do not agree. It means I want to keep it simple.

You are very expressive but when it comes to asking for some help you never do it. Please if you need any help due to mood fluctuations or hormonal changes please say it, as I do not understand the gravity of pain you go through. I cannot read your mind no matter how much you train me.

I am not able to guide you in right way when you want an advice on makeup, the lipstick colour the liners etc. All colours look same to me the thin difference in shades are out of my understanding. I do not know if the thin or thick eye liner suits you. I just like the way you are comfortable with.

It is ok if you want to have that me time; I understand what you do for all of us. The way you take care of everything home is appreciable. I may not say this but you can always order for the ME break and you will get it mam.

Your Loving Husband

STAY AT HOME DAD

Stay at home moms is something we all know, but stay at home dad is someone you must have heard of, or may have someone around you.

It's the biggest career moves one can make. Men are always looked upon as a masculine power that has to work hard and earn for the family.

This is especially for those dads who have turned moms who have taken all the responsibilities of motherhood. When we celebrate Mother's Day we should also ensure that we celebrate those dads who have done all the part of mothers in their absence. I have seen many cases where fathers have proved to be good parents than mothers the way they take care of their child is really worth appreciating. These days' bringing up of child is not only the responsibility of the mother but it is equally balanced by the father. In some cases where fathers have come forward and understood the responsibility of working mothers. Where they accept the challenge of staying at home or working from home this is probably seen in those cases where mother's job is more challenging and demands more attention whereas, in some cases it is more of just an empathy towards mothers. While we say that mothers are not leaving any stone unturned with respect to their demands of job and career, they are giving a tough to men, on the other hand, men are also balancing the same by taking care of kids sharing the burden of parenthood just by being a stay-at-home dad.

We say that dads and mum collectively bring up the children; their way of teaching the child is different. When they both are involved in physical activities with the child dad tries to make the child stronger than the mothers try to make the child more sensitive. Mothers and fathers parent children differently but that is the greatest benefit the child can have.

SAHD's are not homemakers but that is the choice they have made. They encourage the woman to give her a hundred percent in her career and stay more oriented and focused on her responsibilities in the office. Today handing over your baby to a Nanny is of great risk and considering the increasing crime in case of children, having your better half at home to take care of your child is the biggest asset a woman can have.

Today's Lifestyle demands both the parents to be working or say earning, in such cases I would like to share an example of one of my colleagues who was working in a day shift and his wife was working in the night shift it was quite easy for them to handle the child in the absence of another parent. And the child was happy to get the complete attention of each parent when around.

It's not easy to be a SAHD because society around has a different view of looking towards him, people may think that there is a lack of motivation, or even may think he is jobless or in a search of job. Our society till date fails to handle the fact that women are equally out in the corporate world to earn like men and men can also choose to stay at home and manage single-handedly given an opportunity.

Maternity is the biggest phase of a women's life when she decides to give up on her career or to continue with the same giving up on her child's upbringing. I believe SAHD has given the best gift they can give to their women by staying at home and taking care of the child leaving the mother to explore the opportunities rather than leaving her at home for the postpartum depression.

SAHD does all every mother do for the child like taking the child to the park, having a play date, cooking for the child, taking care of the child, regular medical visits vaccines, and checkups, dressing up the child to the best, attending the B-Day parties, school responsibilities of the child, attending the PTM's, eating habits basically all the responsibility that a mother does when she is at home. He does all the house chores the market, purchasing veggies and grocery managing the maids their duties and their salaries everything becomes a part of his life.

To understand it better it is more like the movie Ki and Ka where a man takes care of the entire house being homemaker even wearing the mangalsutra and the woman is the bread earner.

Where we are celebrating Mother's Day for all his duties that a mother does we should not forget this stay at home dads who are the best mum today.

Movies are the reflection of the society we live in. Where some years back we always heard mother oriented songs in movies... Like tu kitni achhi hain... Maa meri maa. In recent years we have movies like Akele him akele tum...oh I love you daddy and....... sabse acha kaun hian papa mere papa.

So this mother's day do not forget to remember and cheer up for those dads who have chosen to stay back and be SAHD.... stay at home dad.

PAGES FROM HIS DAIRY

June 2020

Today I was in mood of cooking something out of the world. When I was bachelor it was my daily task, but since I shifted with mummy and further got married I hardly got chance to show my culinary skills.

Lockdown -It's a long holiday, thou the condition outside house was not really good, all are trying to relax and try hands on different skills and art. Some of my friend have started regular workout and yoga. It a major emergency in world due to pandemic outbreak. We were not able to go out for shopping and so me and my wife decided to use the available stuff at home carefully so that it's sufficient till lockdown opens.

She is doing the entire household except few jobs that I do to help her. The maids are on leave. Today I thought of trying my culinary skills again and surprise her.

I told her to relax and lunch was on me. She was happy with surprise and big question mark.

"What you want to cook? You tell me I will do else my work will increase and I will end up doing more work".

I ensured her she had a day off today. Of course the menu was Chinese her all time favourite.

I insisted her to sit in drawing room and watch television. Handed over the remote to her and here I begin, the new apron and little assistant who was of no use, than simply was bombing questions on me why are you cooking today? Is mummy not well? What are you searching? Wait I will ask mummy? She simply disturbed me and gave me those surprising looks like I was alien in kitchen.

The kitchen is changed, in fact quiet new to me. I asked her where the noodles and sauces are.

She came in and showed me the sauces in shelf right in front of me. I added rice? She opened the cupboard and handed the container.

While she returned back I realised the ginger garlic paste is very important for Chinese. I searched for it in refrigerator and could not find it. I again called her to ask, before I finished my sentence the little monster arrived pointed at a container for the paste.

I asked her to on the music for the chief. I was trying to open the noodles packet while it tore open and scattered all over. I collected them and started chopping the veggies. I love that cutting sound crunchy one….tak takk tak….with my favourite big knife. While the noodles boiled in a new pan and rice cooked I was done with base work.

I gave the tadka and flavoured it with sauces, wow yummy it looked. I decorated the plate served it in a beautiful bone China plate and shut off the exhaust. While I remove the apron I saw it got bit painted with sauces. It is ok it is meant for that and moved to drawing room with the plate.

I fed her with a fork in my hand and to see her expressions sat in front of her. She loved it. I was happy she loved it. We raised a toast for my culinary skills and yummy food.

She was done with her lunch and went to kitchen. No wonder she came back frown and grumbling. Gave me those angry looks and said

"My kitchen was so dull you really got rainbow in it".

Thanks and started collecting the utensils and dishes, with a duster in hand. She wore the apron with signs of my skills on it. Again gave me a look for painting her new apron and moved ahead.

I do not know what went so wrong! As I was trying to help her out and the food really turned out to be good. I think I can cook sometimes may be once in month or so.

She cleaned the kitchen and the white wall which reflected the sauces and all the tadkas I gave. The red chilli sauce, green chilli sauce and yellow turmeric, the soya droplets. She collected chopped capsicum and onion on the kitchen slab. The sink was full of utensils. She has so many utensils I realised. She made the kitchen all clear. Now turning to the refrigerator she cleaned the handle I opened with my oily hands. Finally the kitchen was simply black slab with clean white tiles on it simple black and white. I had almost got the kitchen coloured oh that is what she meant by rainbow.

I do not think she will allow me cook again? But don't I add colours to her plain kitchen life.

Her dairy

Day off from kitchen was not worth, it is better I cook and not let him enter the kitchen and end up doing double the work.

I could count the number of utensils I had in kitchen. Oh god I hope he doesn't make plan to cook every month doing experiments in my kitchen.

THE MELTING PILLAR OF HOUSE

I always wondered how much gifts and cards on special days made difference to my dad. I remember when was in my teens and came to know about the father's day celebration I wrote a letter to him and got it couriered in same city. To my surprise after years I saw the letter in one of his files some days back.

Father's day is celebrated on third Sunday of June to recognise the immense contribution by them in our life.

Not many dads around really know this day, as fathers in India are not used to being celebrated for their status as fathers. For them it is more about their Dharma the responsibility they have, that is what they are suppose to do. So they do have much great expectations about such celebrations in fact they are pretty ok with birthday wishes.

In today's world we have different meaning for celebrations and gifts. But people in earlier generations will share it doesn't much matter to them about their birthday celebrations and all, as they were not much taught about it. They grew up with a thought about their responsibility and their performance.

Let us not forget the Martians chapter we have learned. For this generation it matters only if you try to shrink away your responsibilities. The reason is men are generally raised not to be sentimental, it is now that we encourage them cry and speak out. Else we have always heard our mothers saying, do not cry like a girl! Men are supposed to be strong and tough. Being the pillars and breadwinner of family, they are supposed to act as the pillars. They have jobs to perform which expects them to be 'Macho'.

Sentiments a soft heart tears and outburst are not considered as characteristics of men. They are supposed to take up things and fix it in case of emergency. That what we hear 'Be a Man' Men were always one who had responsibility to keep family safe.

After being a father they are supposed to be more serious and responsible. It's always a mother who take care of children at home and father who deals with everything that is outside the house. It was never a case when men discussed business at home till the last generation.

Things are changing and the pillars are melting, mothers are sharing the responsibility outside home and so dads are sharing inside. It is not only about celebrating mother's day but it is also about celebrating father's day. Gone are the days of keeping business affairs to themselves, now they share it with wife and kids. Men are getting less egoistic. They are equally involved in the child's life like the mother is. They are even part of activities like cooking and nanny business. Far from being detached and aloof today's fathers are keenly involved and attached to their kids.

The number of fathers having household responsibilities is on rise as mothers have started stepping out of house to achieve economic stability. Dad's today are accepting their emotions, sentiments likes and dislikes, let us not judge them or make mistake on their weakness. Today fathers are able to display the strength of being able to express. This has brought the families even closer in real sense.

Gone are the days when children were afraid of their dad as and got a threat from mother saying she will complain to dada once he is back. Dads are more of buddies and equal partners in crime.

Fathers are equally supporting, caring, and considerate just like mothers. So the old age saying "Men will be men" doesn't suit here at least.

It made difference to him but being the responsible and bread earner of the family he was engraved in his duties and did not really mention much about it. Finally this father's day he said Thank you than his typical 'hmm smile' after my wish.

HE IS EXPECTING

ges ago when pregnancy was the only women's responsibility and pain, couple have started evolving saying
'We are Pregnant'. It is not only the wife but the couple
who shares the responsibility for nine months and more.

Women's body features and her overall mindset and bringing up
help her in this phase but for fathers it is not less than surrogacy.
They do not undergo any physical changes and are often get the
left out feeling.

How do you stay involved?? Here are some tips-

Accompanying your wife for all gynacologist appointments, her
yoga classes, her ultrasounds and tests will make you be part of
this phase and feeling. You will get a close association with both
baby and mother.

Reading about pregnancy in books or hearing from friend can be
a good option to explore the phase and the changes occurring.
Learning about the phase may help you and keep yourself prepared for next change.

India being cultural country and having ayurveda background, we believe in Garabha Sanskar. Be part of that phase when you can interact with your child and get bonded even before birth by talking to the baby, playing music sharing things.

Give an ear to your wife as she must be going through different changes, physically as well as some emotionally. Share her experience and help her smoothening down and relaxing.

Mood swings of the expecting mother is something ever man has to suffer, best thing to do here is discuss and leave no misunderstanding between. It is natural reaction but you can avoid it by handling her carefully.

Believe in doctors and do not unnecessary get panic for any health issues of your wife. The professionals are best to take care of it and of course your wife is not the first mother on earth, so do not be anxious.

Once the baby has come, there are lot of changes in life. They need to handle patiently. As restrictions evolve you can overcome them collectively.

Will I be a good father? There are no normal on earth for it, but as you are thinking so you are already a good father.

There are prenatal classes which can be additional thing you opt for if at all you are very anxious.

Learn and help your wife in nappy changing, some house chores, and exercise, take turns to take care of baby. So that she doesn't feel exhausted and you get some time with baby.

Your relationship with wife will change for the best as you have one more life to take care of between you two. While she is not only a wife but a mother too, you not only a husband but a father too.

Enjoy your fatherhood.

NO MORE SECRET SANTA

It was Christmas around the corner and a mail dropped from the corporate office about the game-Secret Santa.

I remember days when in school we all friends used to be excited with Santa Stories. The school used to show us movie in a year based some theme. This year it was new movie home alone. The young little boy was left by his mother all alone at home in Christmas holidays.

One of the friends shared the story of the boy in next division; he got so many gifts last year. Seems he hung his pair of socks with his wish list on the Christmas night. We all were hearing it with surprise and wish to get the gift this year.

After going home I asked my mother, why we do not hang our socks Momma. You know the boy in other division got so many gifts last year.

Momma was not listening to anything I was saying, but still was nodding her head.

Further I added momma but will such fat man come in our house if we closed doors and sleep? Finally she replied you should ask your friends!

Next day again during recess we were discussing about the Santa, I got answer to my question that he manages to come through chimney holes. Now chimney holes in Maharashtra houses in Pune district was out of question. Then we concluded here in our place open window is ok, no matter if there are grills on it, Santa will manage.

While dad was silently watching us do all stuff, he did not much say about it. Finally the day arrived and we hang our socks near the window, such that Santa's hand would touch it.

I was unable to sleep with excitement of Santa's arrival. But somehow did not realise when I fall asleep. Early morning I sat on my bed, without opening my eyes. I rubbed them and moved towards the window. Window was closed, the sight brought tears to my eyes. One more Christmas was gone without gift.

Sadly I sat near my bed, and saw me socks fall down, I picked up the socks and my list of gifts was no more in it. I ran to momma and told her.

Momma seems Santa had come he took away my list and before he could keep the gift for me the window must have closed. Will he come again today as my gift must be with him? What do you think?

She smiled and said get ready for school. I got ready and picked up my bag and water bottle and Tiffin. With lot of questions in my mind I said bye to momma and walked out of house.

A brand new Bicycle was in front of my house. I was wondering, whose it was? It had balloons on it and was decorated.

I went close to it and saw. There was a note of my name and wishing me merry Christmas. I cried and shouted loudly momma momma come fast, see I told you Santa had come and he could not put the cycle in the socks so he kept it here.

Happily I took my cycle to school and now this year it was about me and my Santa story. After couple of days I understood who my Santa was in disguise.

I was very happy to my surprise, my Santa stood front of me in white shirt black pant, no beard and almost half the weight of original one. I hugged my dad.....My no more secret Santa.

That was the last year I had asked Santa for gift, as by next year I understood, the Santa is no one but my dad, who fulfilled my wishes irrespective of Christmas.

I am sure children will make stories out of this and there will be someone like me next year looking for Santa on Christmas Eve.

So getting prepared for secret santa in corporate world, lets play.

FREEDOM FOR MEN

Sounds interesting, yes I guess not many must have really thought about this.

It's a man world isn't it? There is no denying on this fact. But are men free, are they enjoying their freedom. Unlike women, men in every culture, whether Asian, European or Western men have enjoyed their freedom of expression, choice to live their life on their own terms.

Though today women stand equally to men, men are considered the bread winners for the family. He is one who holds the entire responsibility of the family. If we stir in our values men are taught to be the responsible and superior since childhood.

Even today couples or say families insist on male child, and rejoice his birth as he is nothing but their retirement plan. He is best investment for parents, which on maturity gives benefits. It may sound harsh but that is fact behind the idea of raising son in better way than daughters. Have you ever given a thought when parents treat both children equally why is son insisted to be only caretaker 'Budhape ka sahara' and daughter 'a paraya dhan'.

If daughters do not take parents responsibility it is not a shock for society but the moment son holds back his responsibility or refuses to take care of his parents that is cultural shock. Especially in India, sons are born for taking care of parents. I do not deny that now day's daughters too take care of parents but very few. Is not this disparity?

As a child son also dreams of having a carrier out of his interests like singing, dance, art, or sports person. But under the circumstances of holding him responsible for family, being bread earner and the fact that who will be taking care of parents in old age, he cannot experiment with his carrier. He has to have some concrete carrier which has good earning. Where is the **freedom of choice**

Once they are done with taking care of parents further comes interesting second phase Wife, children, and their education and household responsibilities. Many men have given up their interests and taken up the responsibility of family. My father was a professor and was interested in literature and history, but due to sudden death of my grandfather he had to take up farming and responsibility of his young siblings. He slowly forgot his interests and lived every day as it came to earn and take care of family.

They have to choose responsibility over their passion. Is this not a story of every man around? Very few men get the opportunity to explore their interests and take it up as carrier.

They just cannot choose their interests when they have a family to take care of, they cannot opt a carrier for themselves. The funny part is their values in market of marriage is based their salary or income not their talent and skills. Every girl dreams of a prince with the guitar in his hand, but actual prince hardly gets time to learn guitar.

It is believed that the best cooks worldwide are mostly men, but in India thou we love recipes of Sanjeev Kapoor, Ranveer Brar and Vikas Khanna, even Akshay Kumar is a good chef but when in common families like our men cook they get those weird taunts of *Jodu ka Gulaam* or get nagging for mess in kitchen.

Women do take break by visiting their mothers place for rest, they are always considered and are one always pitied on for adjusting to new atmosphere, new house and new family members. They get recharged or say rejunivated after they visit their mothers place for few days. But husband do not have that option they always are the one balancing wife and mother and no matter how hard they try to balance they are tagged mummaz boy and jodu ka gulam. Unfortunately they do not have a place like maika to get recharged or take off from the ladies and responsibilities.

Women feel extreme pride to call themselves papa ki pari but why it is so demeaning to be called mummaz boy? Does this sound like being *freedom from prejudice* .

If women are dominated, oppressed or maltreated we have so much to say on, but when it comes to men and their suffering we easily behave deaf.

We believe every woman when she stands against men for any wrongdoing, we easily believe her version of story than men. While law stand with women all the way, do men really enjoy the *freedom from bias?* While practicing in court for couple of years I have seen how men suffered due to strong legal side women have in law. I have seen women misuse the law for their benefit and ruin men's life.

In the quest to celebrate women hood we at times have been pretty unfair to men .After all, **Freedom from inequality** will come only when both genders are not given equal opportunity but also equal credits.

DO'S AND DON'TS

en also have a list of do and don'ts, we have never discussed how these do's and don'ts are taught to them and how they impact life in long run. We are always the stronger human species on earth irrespective of how soft we are at heart.

The birth of male child is rejoiced and the child is immediately loaded with expectations and responsibilities, not less than Virus-Viru Sahastrabudhhe in Three idiots, who asked the new born if he wants to be footballer.

There is a lot of struggle every man goes thru which cannot go unmentioned

Boys don't cry: From the very beginning boy are told, crying is a weak person's act. They are taught that boys are strong and they do not cry. No matter how critical or bad the situation is they are not supposed to cry. Even we must have seen people taunting men why crying like a girl? They are taught that crying is girl's job as they are weaker.

Time has changes and now society accepts the fact that men even can be sensitive.

Boys do not cook: Thou we have seen the achari's or bawarchi's have always been men, we do not accept them cooking in their own kitchen. There are many men who are world famous cooks and they cook much better than women. Actually no skill is designed for a particular gender. Men are always laughed on if they have a role to play in kitchen, they are often termed 'jodu ka gulam'. The term doesn't make sense as we expect them to be sensitive, help their better half in household and then taunt them.

Boys are the bread earners: Boys are taught right from their birth that they are going to be the bread earners and have to take the responsibility of the house. It is continuously touched upon them that they have to be the leader of the family, a good earner, and chose a carrier where in they can serve all family members.

Thou girls are earning equally or more than boys, no where the taboo of they being responsible for the old and new generation is not rubbed off.

Boys are strong: Boys are always taught that they are strong and have to remain stronger than other gender, irrespective of anything and everything around. They have to be tuff in critical times and give courage to the family. Men are body shamed even for their weak or say thin body structure as it is pre decided that they have to be strong emotionally as well as physically.

Decision making is always done by head of the family and it is always men. They are always responsible for decision making in financial and important matters. As the result of this they are hold responsible for wrong decisions as well.

The point is every responsibility can be taken up by family members, and everybody should be treated equally. When everybody fights for equality for women, we chose to keep silent on this default pressures created on men by society. If we observe the successful women around in society, we will see that they are supported by a concerned and sensitive, caring man in their life. So can we conclude - Behind every successful woman also lies a caring Man.

HOMEMADE SANDWICHES

Apart from pizzas and burgers, my wife and mother collectively cook a fantastic dish-Sandwich. The stuffing, the roasting, cheesing everything is perfect. I just do not like it. Because it is nothing but 'ME'.

At some peak time, I resemble so much to a sandwich , thanks to my mom and my beloved wife. We always get to negotiate with our parents, in-laws, friends and wife. There are so many instances that can be narrated where we are nothing with the stuffing in the sandwich.

Instance one-parents are ever ready to direct or narrate Baghban -2 when they get a feeling that their son is a husband too. They expect instant reply for something they say as a tester-like I had a bad day, if I do not revert it is understood that she – mom is calculating on my response to my wife and has to say an essay on it, as to how my revert to my wife is of concern and how I am least bothered to them. That's a story every alternate day. Now why will dad stay away from this, he has to be the part of it once I am out this doubles game. Every three to four days he has to say a classic all time favourite line "I wonder what will happen with your mother after me". They keep making that poor guy faces for sons to melt.

Parents find out way to steal those few hours at home. Dad used to bang the door a hard the moment we are off to the room to sleep. It was just to apply a pain relief gel on his back. Not only this, but Mom did the same early morning to wake us up. That is where the sandwich preparations start.

Further these sandwich moments add in your life and are there forever.

Solution and best thing to do is take a clam look, chill pill on it. Do not react and carry on. In laws are also ` parts of this occasionally on the special days and celebrations at times.

The younger sibling at home becomes an endangered species when his elder brother becomes a husband. Now they are not the part of every discussion so they feel free to call themselves outsider. Now the younger sibling becomes parents pet and the only loving and concerned son.

Friends are one you can discuss and try to get solution as they also sail in same boat at some moment of time. We also find solace when we narrate the aap biti to them. Finally after bunch of solution to various issues, none of them actually works, thou are tested and failed.

A lot can happen over a cup of tea or coffee, we friends sit discuss and try to find an equilibrium which can never be attained. Slowly the discussion goes on rocks with no solution….cheers. An important role I play is to design a holiday package for wife. No matter how you plan for parents they just do not leave house out of the fear or losing it once for all. And the moment she plans her in laws wants her to cancel it or return soon. This gives a feeling of getting married to in laws and their son.

A friend shared his parents get more than happy when they know their DIL is planning to go to her mother's place. That is a planned holiday for them.

We as husbands are looked upon as a problem solving machine, to problems which do not exist. We have constant sense of responsibility along with us everywhere we go. When the world had to say lot on women getting married and going thru lot, same applies to us men too as no matter what we have that constant sense of responsibility of balancing and reaching the equilibrium to see-saw.

There is no solution than just planning your days and time right with everybody in family.

Further frequently toppings are added to these sandwiches and enjoyed with sauces.

BE A MAN

I heard this first time when Aamir khan said it to Saif Ali Khan in Dil Chahata Hain, remember? I remember the scene where in Aamir wants Saif to be bit stronger and dominating against his head strong girlfriend. Is it that the men are supposed to be, just being dominating and stronger makes you a man?

Today , when I taught my pre-primary kid to write the word MAN and was trying to make her understand it. I was also making myself bring clarity on it. Thou she now identifies man in pictures. I gave it a thought of what exactly "Be a Man" means.

Let us understand how we look at man. Earlier role of man and women were defined and different.

Today the roles have mixed up as both of them share same responsibilities, they go to office, they cook they take care of children. There are no role cut down to men and women. Earlier it was defined which to some extent has changed now. They collectively share the responsibility of the house may it be changing diapers or cooking, taking care of children or even being parent at home. The couple of the house has to define and have role play for better understanding of their children to be a man. They have to team up with kids and decide on, what are the action and character traits they want their child to inculcate.

Men are always considered strong, physically as well as mentally; this may act as pressure on kids. If they excel athletically it is acceptable but when they fall short for it becomes a struggle. Many times boys are judged on their performance or how they look in the field. If we can't judge a girl based how she makes food or rotis. Similarly, you can't judge boys based their performance on field. We should treat them equally and not always insist on winning. We should appreciate the kid for participating and playing a game and accept his failure so that our sons know it is ok to lose.

 It is not important to be gentlemen as it is to be a polite caring and concerned person. One should always treat other with respect, try and help others, this is not because you are a man but you are polite person. You can always help and serve not only ladies if anyone who needs help. That is what real men do. One should be able listen respectfully to anyone's thoughts or decisions and disagree or reject politely. Real man may be strong but he needs to be polite.

It is ok to be scared of or be vulnerable when needed, that is a human trait. It is ok if you fail and even okay to admit things when they are wrong. You need to be honest about your feelings and need not have the brave mask every time. It is acceptable to be vulnerable, helpless or even feel scared. When you accept your feeling of being scared you can work on it.

One should be able to see beyond man made differentiations like caste creed, colour, gender, and many more stereotypes created by the society we live in. He should be able to peep in the person's abilities while making important decisions like choosing bride, promoting his junior, choosing members of the team. He should be able to see at one's ability than the outer or cosmetic appearances. As inner beauty abilities and strength outshines the outer appearances.

Dads play a very important role in making of the son. As no matter how much mother trains him he follows his dad. Father sets first example in front of his son, when it comes to behaviour as fathers are role model for sons than their mothers. The father behaviour at home his wife and ladies around reflects his personality and plays vital role in teaching the child as to how women should be treated.

The child closely observes his father's behaviour to his mother, sister, neighbours or daughter. Child doesn't argue or categorise it into good or bad, he believes in what he sees around. Respecting a woman is one of important traits of being a man. It is believed many men change once they have a daughter. Can we teach our sons to be better human than waiting for him to have daughter to change his attitude towards women.

Sometimes it is about too much of unnecessary burden just because they are men. Real men are not born, they are to be moulded and taught in various ways.

Being a man is much more than just being dominating and strong headed. It is about being concerned, being more polite and being good human being as well.

NOT THE MAN'S WORLD

I am blessed with a loving wife and caring mother. I am never made to get up early and make my own tea, or struggle to feed myself. I m a lucky to get the warm cup of tea in my bed followed by ready breakfast. I sometimes invaded kitchen to fetch ice from the freezer or get my part of desserts. You can call me typical middle class Indian man. Women of the house my momma earlier and now my wife do take care of all essential and house chores. Like any other typical man I go to office and return tired. It never strike me, how my momma or wife managed it ,till one evening it happened.....year 2020 changed my life upside down and things are so different as of now. If anyone would have narrated my future I would have called him a bluff master. March 22 the lockdown was announced due to pandemic situation across the country. The discussions on dining table were out of uncertainty around, uncertainty of life and survival, jobs. My wife being associated with the essential services had no option than visiting her clinic every day. And of course I was not required to travel or attend office as corporate had not defined yet about the way of working. My Wife had to attend her clinic, there was no house help available. I had to do visit kitchen more than any other time in my life. I was in a world I never knew! In few hours I realised its women's world. Everything around was new for me, Colourful powders in different containers, various grains number of different spatulas, Some grains I saw only after they were cooked....I stand in kitchen and look around. Eighty percent of things were new to me, I have never seen, never used. I know many of you will connect to me.

I cook dal chawal now, thou they are over cooked and bit liquid form sometimes my family throw no tantrums. My first morning call doesn't go to anyone else than my beloved mumma, who guides me cooking and sharing her recipes. They have saved me many times as not my wife but kids they have prominent nose and taste buds.

Lockdown was an eye opener for me. I started waking up early and rushing to kitchen-the alien territory. I had approached kitchen hardly three times a year so far to cook something.

Cooking is a life skill and everyone should know it irrespective of the gender, age and marital status.

Laundry I never thought had so much variety in it. Washing colour and white clothes differently. Which detergent to use, how much quantity to be used. Thanks to directions of use on the products. It took time to decode the use of detergents, after wash, bleach, ala, and much more.

There is nothing so exhausting like Jaadu Pocha, it is like a vigorous workout. I wish I could have thought of this day when I bought a big house.

Cleaning dishes is like never ending job. I just hate it.

My wife never did finance management but she managed the monthly finances so well. I could not figure out how many rotis we need a day? So how much flour is to be bought, again the variety confused me. Worst was other grocery it made me mad.

Many would suggest why not make list, but to write in list was another question. I randomly visited the grocery store and picked up everything in knew, unfortunately that was not all required and important.

Finally wife prepared the list and gave, which really saved time and me.

The lockdown as being big learning curve for me. I realised how relaxed my life was away from all this things and how did my she – my wife manage all this stuff without complaining.

I worked, attended office all 365 days, when I needed holiday I took one, I went on tours and holiday to relax. But managing house was much of running an 24 hours institution.

I would urge everyone to take a step and help their better halves in small ways to do household. Try to be man who is known for taking up his responsibility of the house not only by attending office but at home also doing households

Sharing is caring. Let us use it the other way by sharing respon-sibilities by taking some. Else thou all say it's a man's world, it is actually women's world we are running through.

READING BETWEEN THE LINES

Men are always compared with women on every ground, may it be looks, physical appearance, habits, feeling and much more. It is always said that it is difficult to understand women and what is in her mind. It may be an illusion in what you see and she means.

The fact is there is much more to what men say and do like women. You will discover illusion here to.

The art of understanding men is required specially when they sound very much normal. When a man is husband his words mean different that they actually mean, like he means yes when he says no, and vice versa.

When they say 'Yes' they mean it except they are asked for shopping or exercise. They give the expected answer to make us happy. What they really mean is no, they want to say NO. So let us understand when they are masking no Behind YES.

"Kids stayed back so well, they did not trouble, and in fact I think I do this job very well than you".

Now that's big lie. He uses such explanations to cover up what he went thru when you were not around. He will assure you he is super dad, the best when it comes to babysitting.

He will never admit how bad his day was with kids thou he must have lost it many times during the day.

When he says you look slim in this dress, he may sometimes say this just to please you and make you happy, which is acceptable. He may not always like your choice but agrees on it to make you feel good and confident.

A women becomes a mother when she goes thru immense pain and emotions, but the person standing beside's her who feels responsible for it is the father. He doesn't understand what's happening!! They are unable to put their emotions to words, and of course they are not allowed to cry.

Most of the men are not those chocolate boys like their wives expect them to be. Every girl dreams of Rajesh Khanna, Amitabh, Vinod Khanna, Shashi and Rishi.....to Shahrukh and Ranbir.

The three words come as simple to them as dramatically it comes in movies. Just Plain and simple. Some try make it as per their loves wish. This is the way they are, men are not very expressive, they fall short of words and expressions. They can't speak it.

 Men shop a lot, they are not fond of shopping but yes they shop everything and anything. They may not take long for choice but they take everything they do not really need. Try and recall the last shopping.

More than women now a day's men try all the cosmetics. Roles have changed women are trying to have more natural and raw look and men trying the cosmetics, Why not? They also want to dress up look good. They also have grooming kits. Now that men have taken over the fairness products, they are getting fair, fairer. Like women they also have different bags, valet, dresses, night creams, day creams, moisturisers, beard oil, perfumes etc etc.

If you call them, you are disturbing. If they call you, they are missing you.

If you advice, you are dominating, if they advice it's their care for you.

If you talk when they drive, you drive them crazy. When they speak, while you are driving they are just being concerned again.

That is the way they are so identical like we women are.

THE JOURNEY OF DACOIT TO SAINT

The story is journey of a man from an dacoit to a saint. He is one who wrote the great and first Epic "Ramayana". He is the first poet of the universe.

A robber or say a dacoit Valya used to hide roadsides and rob the travellers. In due course he also had to kill many of them who refused to give way their belongings. It was Valyas way of feeding his family.

He used to rob people take away the belongings and serve his family. In case he had to kill the traveller he used to put a stone in pot. Months and years passed him doing so. There were lots of pots filled with stones.

One day Maharishi Narad was passing by, while valya attacked him and asked him give away his belongings. Narad had nothing to lose. Her carried a Veena with him. He offered his veena to Valya saying he doesn't have anything else to give away.

Narad offered him to kill him, but still he doesn't hold anything apart from Veena to give away. Valya was not interested in Veena. Further Narad asked him why the pots were filled with stones. Valya told him they were the murders he did till date. He told him he shared the belongings with his family and that was only earnings they get.

Narad asked him so your family shares whatever you get from the travellers, so they must be sharing the sins also.

Valya did not understand what sins were, after Narad explained him that hurting and killing people is nothing but sin and he can lead a better life. If he at all he is doing this for his family his family should also share the sins, along with the benefits of robbery.

Narad questioned him, oh so by doing so you have so much of Paap-Sins done, valya said no issues as his family was with him everywhere in sins also. Narada asked him if he was sure he family will accompany him to hell and punishments he would get because of these sins?

Valya was sure, but Narad confused him to the extent that he approached his family and asked his wife and children if they would share the sins along with the benefits they got from robbery and murdering people. His wife and children denied the sins straight away.

Valya felt very sad, speechless and returned to Narad saying his family was not ready to share the sins. Narad explained him the fact of life. Valya cried out his heart felling sorry as he was taken aback by his wife's and children's answers. He begged the Narada to guide him to the right path of leading life.

Narad suggested him to chant god's name and meditate to understand the real meaning of life. Valya was so much into killing people he could not chant the words RAM. Narad asked him if he can chant MARA, to which Valya replied yes he can.

While he started chanting Mara Mara Mara...it became Rama Rama Rama. Years passed and Valya kept meditating the name of Lord Rama. He was engraved in the chanting that he did not realise an anthill that surrounded him.

One day Narada blessed him, removed the anthill around him and opened his eyes. He guided him to form an ashram and give teachings to people around.

Over a period of Valya came to known as Valmiki and wrote Ramayana. If we visit the place Valhe we still find his pots filled with stones, which converted Valya to Valmiki.

We have different personality traits, characters within us. We need to sharpen our skills and choose the right trait to live a good life.

KNIGHT IN SHINING ARMOURS

Deep inside every man is brave hero. He wants to succeed in serving and protecting his family in odd times. He wants to be appreciated admired as a hero. He becomes more caring when he is trusted and appreciated for his deeds. He feels more encouraged and confident. He feels lost and discouraged if he loses his energy. He doesn't like anyone to guide him, or give solutions.

Here is a story

A knight in shining armour was travelling through the countryside. Suddenly he hears a woman crying a waiting for someone to save her. She is trapped by a dragon.

He urges his horse to the gallop and races to the castle to save her. He pulls his sword and slays the dragon to death. He is lovingly accepted by the princess.

He is rejoiced by the princess, her family and the village. He feels empowered and encouraged. He is accepted and acknowledged as hero, obliviously the princess falls in love with him.

Some days later when, he was out the dragon again attacks the castle. The princess was caught up and caged by the dragon. She starts calling out for help, when he heard her on the way home. He rushes to free her.

He takes out his sword to kill the dragon when the princess shouts do not use the sword use the noose. He listens to her. She instructs him how to use it, he follows her instructions and kills the dragon. His victory is again celebrated but he doesn't feel happy about it. As it was not something he accomplished on his own. He doesn't feel worthy of the villagers trust and celebration. He is slightly depressed and forgot to shine his armour.

A month later when he was leaving for some trip he doesn't carry his sword. She reminds him of the noose and the instruction of using it. On the way home he finds a dragon attacking the castle, he rushes with his sword but hesitates using it. Now he is confused about using the sword or the noose. While he was thinking and making up his mind he the dragon breathes fire and burns his right arm.

He looks up with agony while the princess was waving towards him asked him to us the poison. She throws the poison at him. He smartly poured it in the dragon's mouth and the dragon dies.

Everybody is happy with his bravery of killing the dragon, but he feels incomplete and does not deserve the celebration. He feels discouraged as it was her who saved him. He feels ashamed.

Few months later while the armour was travelling he heard other women shouting and crying for help. He took his sword and for a minute got confused if he should use sword, noose or the poison. He thinks for while what would the princess suggest in such case. He feels sorry and thinks he carries only sword before he met the princess.

He feels confident again throws off his noose and poison. He killed the dragon with his sword and frees the princess. The princess is happy and the village rejoices and celebrates his victory.

He never returns to his princess stays there happily.

In every man is a shining armour who appreciates caring and assistance but too much of it lessens his confidence and turns him off.

Do not try to change your shining armour the way you want, let him take his decisions and have priority. He may feel unloved had you do not accept him the way he is. Even he needs your admiration and encouragement.

Men do not want to be improved.

FATHER IN FATHER IN LAW

Every lady faces a pain of leaving her house after marriage, but more painful is leaving her parents especially father. He is the first man on earth who loved her to no boundaries, who always stood by her against all odds.

Father in law is another father figure you have to live with. It takes time to unfold every relation and would be difficult if you keep comparing any man on earth to your father.

I was almost on clouds like every girl is when she is about to be a bride. While I was ending my spinsterhood my new life was peeping in all newzz. New city, new relations, and a new role. Everything was getting converted legally in law... every relation now had that as a suffix. Daughter-in-law, mother-in-law, father-in-law brother –in-law etc. I was legally doing shopping now and no one was stopping me. I had so many thoughts about what I will wear and how I will present myself, prepare myself for a new phase of my life.

I met my in-laws when they had been to my place. A car stopped at our gate, while we directed to park it inside the compound, a seventy-year-old royal personality got down from the car. He was in blue formals with no cresses on it and black shiny shoes. His white hair shined with the glow of his life's experience. He walked with pride followed by my Mother in law and his son. He had those sharp moustache turned upwards called Handlebar Moustache. Retired from a Bank he had that slow and steady but prompt ascent and choice of words while he spoke. During the very first interaction, he asked me many questions but one I remember was do you cook non-veg or are only fond of eating? followed by a sweet and mischievous smile. His love for non-veg easily reflected from his question. He was very polite and used more of the English language while he spoke, being more expressive and comfortable in English.

While they were about to leave he got a shoe hand from his car door cavity. It reflected their hygiene importance in life which normally gets ignored by that age. I really admired them for it.

I was shopping I was in discussion with my mother in law for the choice of colours or their preference. Thou I was keen on my choices I was trying to understand their preference and culture as well. While I was very much in discussion with my mother in law, I hardly spoke to my father in law. One day he grabbed the phone and asked me why did I did not talk to him often as I did with my Mother in law.

I had no answer for it, but I just explained it that I was discussing shopping and she was the better one to answer those queries. Getting an opportunity to talk, I asked him, what should I call you?

He Said, Have you heard of Alexander and Porus? I replied positively. He further added when Alexander had caught Porus, he asked Porus how do I treat you. To which Porus replied "Treat me as a king would treat with another King"
So treat me as you treat your father, what do you call him? I answered Papa. He further added so you can call me 'Papa'.
I found a father in Father in law while I stood in selecting a Sari for my grand occasion.
My first interaction with him as a daughter in law was very memorable, what was yours?

THE SACRIFICE
OF THE KING

He was a son of a great Maratha king, was something I knew about him a two decades ago. Thanks to my Delhi Board schooling which surprisingly did not include any Maratha history.

One fine Sunday I had an historic outing with a friend of mine to Tulapur, I hardly remember this name heard few times. Tulapur is a village in Pune District, on the banks of three rivers Bhima, Bhama and Indrayani, hence called Triveni sangam. This place is associated with last moments of Sambhaji Maharaj.

It is known for the black day in the history of Maratha Samrajya as the Second Chhatrapati of the Marathas Shri Sambhaji Maharaj was killed by Mughals.

A statue of the brave warrior stood before us, while I reached the place, I could feel something in the air which was painful. While I looked at the statue with chin up, I could read the history of the place on the walls.

Sambhaji Raje was brought to Tulapur and tortured and executed by Mughal forces. Sambhaji Raje with handful of soldiers could have escaped knowing the Mughals had attacked, with the help of his own Brother in law Shirke, but he fought bravely and unfortunately got imprisoned. Along with him his friend and poet Kavi Kalaash was also imprisoned. It is believed that Kaavi Kalaash also died due to Aurangzeb's torture but the King suffered for 40 days.

They were tortured to extent of brutality .their eyes, nails and skin was plucked off. They were not provided food. Their eyes were removed and salt sprinkled on the bare skinless body. He was asked to accept Islam and burned with hot rods on refusal.

Finally, on the 40th day when Sambhaji Raje was asked to surrender his forts, treasures. He was repeatedly asked to accept Islam, to his refusal his tongue was pulled off, on putting the question again he wrote "Not even if the emperor bribed me with his daughter" which led to his death.

It was 11 March 1689, when the brave warrior, the king was killed brutally at the age of 31. He was killed by cutting into pieces and thrown into river, beheading and tearing apart his body front and back with the tiger claws and even feeding to dogs. His suffering and pain was put into words by Kavi Kalash and is carved on the walls at Tulapur.

Kavi Kalash Samadhi is also in the same premises.

Further, it is believed that Sambhaji Maharaj remains were collected by Patil's, stitched together for his last rites. The act gave the Patil's the position as Veche Patil (One who collected) and Shive Patil (One who stitched). Further the stitched body was cremated as per Hindu rituals at Wadbudruk.

There is a Samadhi built at a Wadbudruk also as a memory of this painful event.

Shocked with the reality of the history of a great Maratha warrior I further read "Sambhaji" by Vishwas Patil which brought clarity and added knowledge.

Sambhaji Maharaj was equally stronger and intelligent like his father the great Maratha warrior Shivaji Maharaj. He was the king of the Maratha Empire, a scholar of Sanskrit language, a good poet, a brave warrior; he had good knowledge on Nitishastra, Hindu Jurisprudence and Puranas. He was extremely brave to the extent that he would tear apart tiger all alone. So renowned as Chhava-the Cub.

In young age he lost his mother and got his childhood lessons from his grandmother - Jijabai and father the great Maratha King-Chhatrapati Shivaji Maharaja when they were in Nazar Kaid and freed themselves from the Agra Fort by the famous 'Ganimikava'.

Today Many youngsters participate in 'Sambhaji Maharaj Balidan Mass' means Sambhaji Maharaj Sacrifice month where in they fast for 40 days in memory of his sacrifice, they do not wear shoes and follow it equivalent to any pious month. The youngsters sacrifice their favourite foods and walk all the way which is called MUKH PADA YATRA. The sacrifice of a young warrior and the great Maratha King is still mourned on in various parts of Maratha Empire.

A PROMISE TO PROTECT

Shishupal was born with three eyes and four arms, there was an akashvani from heaven saying his extra organs would fade way or say disappear when some person would take him in his lap, but the same person would be one who would kill Shishupal.

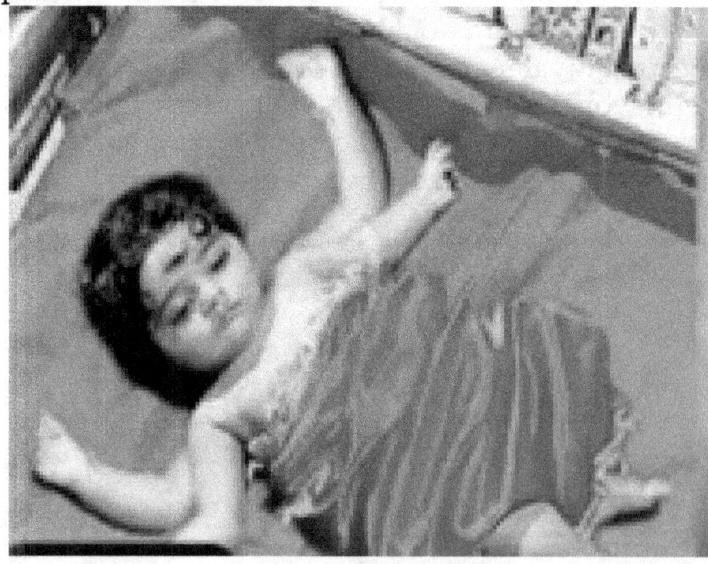

Shishupals mother was very worried and scared of every person who visited them. One day her brothers son Krishna when took Shishupal on his lap and his third eye and two limbs disappeared. Looking at this Shishupals mothers wondered why Krishna would kill him. She begged Krishna to pardon him and give a promise that he would never kill Shishupal. Krishna somehow could not promise this, but he then promised that he would pardon his 100 sins and not kill him. Shishupals mother was satisfied with his promise.

Further years passed and Shishupal held a healthy life. He wished to marry Rukmini his friends sister, but Rukmini with her wish was ran away by Krishna. This made Shishupal hate Krishna.

Here Yudishthir had a ceremony at Indraprastha were Shishupal was invited. It was decided that Krishna would be the honoured guest for the sacrificial ceremony.

Shishupal did not like this and obviously that triggered his anger. He started insulting Krishna and called him mere cowherd and not worth to be honoured. In the flow of his anger he insulted Bhishma as well calling his vow an act of cowardice. Bhishma threatened Shishupala but Krishna Calmed him down and let Shishupal commit his 100th sin to be pardoned.

The next sin was 101th for which he had no pardon. Krishna got angry, released his Sudarshana Chakra and killed him.

In due process Krishna finger got hurt and started bleeding. Draupadi in no moment tore apart her pallu and tied it to Krishna Finger. I t was a big day for Draupadi as she was going to be declared the queen. Her kindness won Krishna's heart.

Krishna promised Draupadi that he would pay off her every thread at right time in the right way.

During Draupadi vastra Haran, Krishna's promise to Draupadi was paid off by offering her never ending saree draped around her.

He kept his word – His promise.

KNOWING MEN

Like it is difficult to understand women for the other gender it's equally difficult to understand men. But some basic readings and difference in men and women's thought and behavioural patterns helps us understand them to some extent. Men and women have complains and thus we share them with relevant people around. When it comes to women they love to speak about problems and need someone to hear them. Here men think women need advice and starts giving solution which women do not need at all.

Men don't like to discuss about their problems they prefer not discussing but thinking all alone curling up around themselves, like entering a cave all alone and coming out after getting some solution with same spirit.

Men are typically like Mr. Fix it known for their solution offering for everything that looks like problem around them.

They are like rubber bands when it comes to relations they stretch to possible limits and get back to place, like pulling back themselves. This pulling back makes women feel left out or lonely.

Men always do things to develop their skills and power. Men love to dress up as per their skills and competence like Police, Soldiers, Businessman, and Scientists, even a cab driver, postman and technicians all wear uniforms. Which reflects their competence and the power the ability of doing specific job?

Men believe in jobs that have actions like hunting, fishing racing cars or say sports. They do not need self help books or magazines much like women. Men are preoccupied with things that express power like powerful cars, gadgets, and powerful technology. For men they love to achieve things so that they feel accomplished and achieve goals. Autonomy is symbol of efficiency power and competency for them.

When she needs care he needs trust, when she wants him to understand, he expects acceptance from her. She expects respect when on the other hand they expects appreciation. He expects admiration but she needs only devotion. He expects validation she expects approval. There is basic difference in their thought process expectations and way of looking and thinking about things.

Deep inside every man is strong hero, a knight in shining armour. He believes in succeeding and protecting his women and his family.

THANKS FOR READING
THE BOOK.

ABOUT THE AUTHOR

Shirish Pawar

Author is a Human resource consultant, Law graduate and Masters in Business Administration worked with MNC's as an HR professional almost for two decades. Currently engaged in training activities for corporates and professional services like designing development courses for kids.

She is a multifacet personality whose journey from carrier oriented girl to the stay at home mom enabled her to express and collect her thoughts on this topic. She is avid reader and blogger too. She expresses on various happenings in society through her blogs on www.meshirish.com

BOOKS BY THIS AUTHOR

Oh!! Womaniya

The collection of interesting and humourous stories about various phases of womens life. It revolves around the most adorable topics of women's life like husband,kids,parents,job,in laws and most importantly LOST her.With funny anectodes and witty tips the author had tried to give you solutions on it. You will definately feel that the author has stepped in your shoes & is narrating your story .You will enjoy sitting back and reading it. It is the journey we all have been thru. The stories will make you smile and feel confident and empowered. Author speaks about women in the past,present and future.
The book will act as aguide,entertainer and storyteller.You will love to gift it to someone who is the "would be" women.The best part is the book suits all groups.
It is warm empathetic A MUST READ BOOK for all

Immortal Teachings

The idea of writing these stories is nothing but to benefit the readers. Some of these stories were heard in school or some in corporate trainings.
Human being is a teacher and the student himself. I would not restrict this book to any age as the stories with morals are the immortal teacher's.
We were students when we heard these stories in schools and today we read this for our children, Stories play important role in shaping the next generations, making them understand our

values.
Stories with morals do wonders with children of all ages, they engage them in imagination and creativity. The stories here are designed short for child to keep focused on it